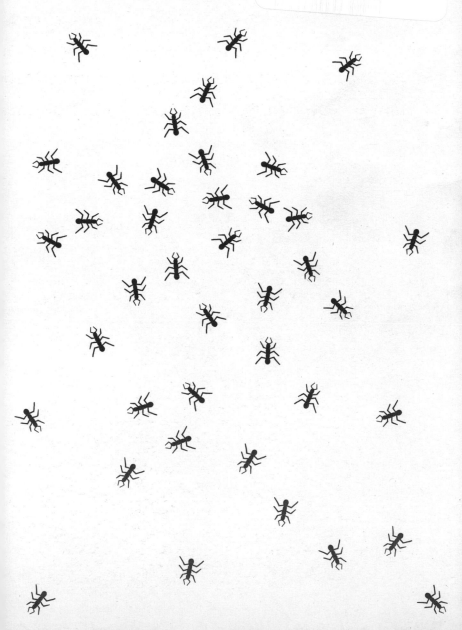

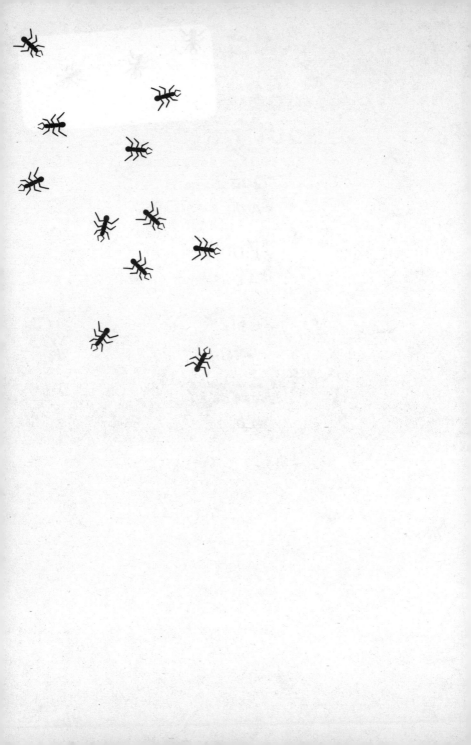

Some words about nature:

"Quack!"
A duck

"Moo!"
A cow

"Bark!"
A dog

A bear

"Squeak!"
A mouse

"Hissssss!"
A tent

More Daisy adventures!

Kes Gray

DAISY

and the trouble with

NATURE

RED FOX

RED FOX

UK | USA | Canada | Ireland | Australia
India | New Zealand | South Africa

Red Fox is part of the Penguin Random House group of companies
whose addresses can be found at global.penguinrandomhouse.com.

www.penguin.co.uk
www.puffin.co.uk
www.ladybird.co.uk

Penguin
Random House
UK

First published 2020

001

Edited by Natascha Biebow at Blue Elephant Storyshaping
Text design by Janene Spencer
Printed in Great Britain by Clays Ltd, Elcograf S.p.A.

A CIP catalogue record for this book is available from the British Library

ISBN: 978-1-782-95771-3

All correspondence to
Red Fox, Penguin Random House Children's
One Embassy Gardens, New Union Square
5 Nine Elms Lane, London SW8 5DA

To Poppy, Daisy, Zoe and Euan

CHAPTER 1

The **trouble with nature** is, there isn't any! At least there isn't any nature in our new school nature garden.

If you ask me, a new school nature garden should be full of nature. AND GARDEN. There should be leaves and grass and flowers and trees and animals and birds and insects and tadpoles and all kinds of different things for children to look at and stroke. All we've got in our new school nature garden is MUD! And all we've got around the mud is BRICKS! There isn't a fox or a squirrel or a daffodil in sight. There isn't even a flea! And it's already been there for A WEEK! If our new school nature garden had been full of nature, then there is no way I'd be having to write a hundred *I must not* lines on the whiteboard. I'd be outside in the playground with my friends, stroking badgers. WHICH ISN'T MY FAULT!

"Build it and they will come," Mr Copford said during his special nature-garden-opening speech in the playground a week ago.

Gabby got really excited. I got really excited. In fact, our whole school had already been excited for a whole entire week because it had taken that long for the builder to build it!

That's the **trouble with bricks**. Before you can put anything inside them you have to make them into walls.

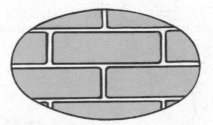

When the builder first wheeled his wheelbarrow into our playground two weeks ago, no one had any idea what he was going to be building. Because he wouldn't tell us. Because it was a secret.

By the end of that week, we still didn't know what he had actually built, even though the brick bits had all been finished and the cement was completely dry.

"Please tell us what it's going to be!" we said.

"I've been sworn to secrecy," said the builder.

"If you tell us what it's going to be, we promise we won't tell anyone," we fibbed.

"Can't do, I'm afraid," said the builder. "I'm not allowed to tell."

"If you tell us what it's going to be, we'll give you a Haribo," we said.

"Uh-uh," said the builder, though he still ate our Haribo.

"If you tell us what it's going to be, we'll give you our tennis ball," we said.

"My lips are sealed," said the builder.

That's the **trouble with builders**. They are really good at keeping secrets. Even if you offer them everything you've got.

"Maybe it's going to be a swimming pool," said Paula Potts.

"It's far too small to be a swimming pool," I said. "Plus if it was a swimming pool it would have ladders going down on the inside."

"Maybe it's a Jacuzzi!" said Gabby. "Imagine if it's going to be a Jacuzzi, with warm water and bubbles for us to relax in!"

"It would still need a ladder," I said.

 "Maybe it's going to be a detention centre," said Jack Beechwhistle. "Maybe they are going to put a big iron grille over the top of the bricks, with a lift-up iron door and a massive padlock. So when any of us get

detention, instead of having to stay in class during break time, we get thrown into the brick pit instead – a bit like a prison or a dungeon."

"Only in a playground instead of a castle," said Harry.

"With torture instruments included," said Colin.

"And live rats," said Jack Beechwhistle.

When everyone arrived back at school after the weekend, it was even harder to tell what had been built for us, because the builder wasn't there any more, plus

there were two big sheets covering up
the bricks.

"There's going to be
an unveiling ceremony
after morning assembly,"
said Barry Morely.

"What's an unveiling ceremony?"
I asked.

"It's when the sheets get pulled off,"
said Gabby. "And everyone gets to
see what the builder has actually built
for us."

Lots of children, including me
and Gabby, wanted to have a peep
under the sheets *before* the unveiling
ceremony, but we couldn't because

11

the sheets were being guarded by a teacher at each end.

The **trouble with sheets being guarded by a teacher at each end** is, everyone had no choice but to wait. And wait and wait and wait.

"Maybe it's a sandpit," said Daniel McNicholl.

"Schools aren't allowed sandpits any more," said Sanjay Lapore, "because cats do poos in them."

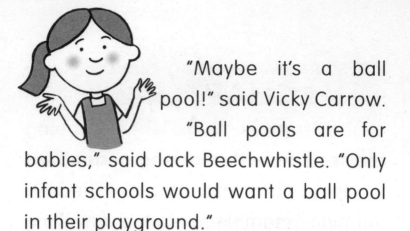 "Maybe it's a ball pool!" said Vicky Carrow.

"Ball pools are for babies," said Jack Beechwhistle. "Only infant schools would want a ball pool in their playground."

"I love ball pools!" said Gabby.

"Me too," I agreed.

So did everyone actually, including Colin and Harry. They were just too much on Jack's side to admit it.

"We'll find out after morning assembly," said Barry Morely. "After assembly, all will definitely be revealed!"

CHAPTER 2

The **trouble with morning assemblies** is, they can take ages. Especially morning assemblies before an unveiling ceremony.

Last Monday's morning assembly wasn't like normal assembling at all. First we had to assemble in our classroom and walk all the way to the assembly hall. Then, when we got to the assembly hall, we had to assemble standing up, then we had to assemble sitting down, then we had to assemble saying a prayer with our eyes closed, then, when a total stranger walked into the assembly hall, we had to assemble standing up again, then we had to assemble sitting down, then

we had to assemble saying good morning to Mrs Jennings, the chairperson of our Parent–Teacher Association, then we had to stay assembled listening to what time

16

the unveiling ceremony would be, and where it would be (but not what the unveiling ceremony would be unveiling), then we had to keep staying assembled sitting down listening to loads more boring assembly stuff, then we had to assemble standing up again, then we had to assemble singing a song about kindness, then assemble sitting down again, then assemble standing up again, and then assemble all the way back to our classroom. Honestly, it was just one assemble after another.

By the time we assembled in the playground for the unveiling ceremony, I was almost dying of excitement.

So was Gabby, so was Paula, so was everyone.

That was *before* Mr Copford and Mrs Jennings lifted the sheets.

"Children, as head teacher of this school, it gives me great pleasure to welcome Mother Nature into our playground," said Mr Copford, standing right next to the bricks. Well, what we could see of the bricks.

"Who's Mother Nature?" whispered Paula Potts, looking around to see where Mother Nature was.

"She's Father Nature's wife," I whispered back.

"She's invisible," whispered Gabby,

nudging Paula to make her stop looking
around while Mr Copford was talking.

"Mother Nature is our greatest blessing," continued Mr Copford. "We can find her all around us in the song of a bird, the hum of a bumblebee, the rustle of a leaf and the sway of a mighty oak. She is the green of our fields, the blue of our skies, the flash of a kingfisher's wing, and now, from this day on, she will, in time, become an ever-present feature of our playground too . . . Mrs Jennings, will you kindly help me do the honours?"

As soon as Mr Copford said "do the honours", everyone held their breath.

"We declare our new school nature garden OPEN!" said Mr Copford.

"Our new ORGANIC nature garden,"
said Mrs Jennings.

The **trouble with someone saying "OPEN"** is, the instant you hear the word "OPEN", you feel like you need to clap.

So everyone clapped.

Except no one knew why they were clapping.

"Where IS the nature?" Gabby whispered in my ear. "I can only see mud."

"Where's the nature?" everyone whispered in everyone's ears.

They could only see mud too.

Gabby could only see mud.

I could only see mud.

Everyone could only see mud.

No one could see any nature at all. There wasn't a bird or a bee or a leaf or a mighty oak or a kingfisher to be seen.

"There may not be much to see now, children, but be patient," Mr Copford told us. "Build an organic nature garden, give Mother Nature time to establish herself, and I promise you that, in time, nature will surely come!"

CHAPTER 3

The **trouble with nature surely coming** is, ours totally didn't.

"The mud must have come at the weekend," said Gabby as we walked back to our classroom after the unveiling ceremony.

"I wish they'd put some nature in with it," I said, sitting down at my desk. "I hate waiting."

"That is the pantsest nature garden in the entire universe," said Jack Beechwhistle, slumping into his chair and folding his arms. "There's more nature in the Sahara Desert than there is in our school nature garden!"

"How long do you think it will take for nature to come?" asked Gabby.

"I don't know," I said. "Let's have another look at break time."

The **trouble with break time** is, you have to do lessons before you can do break time. Luckily, we'd missed a lesson during the unveiling ceremony, so we only had one lesson to go.

As soon as the break-time bell went, everyone rushed back out to the playground to see if nature had come yet.

But it hadn't. The mud looked exactly the same.

"It hasn't even got grass on it," said Stephanie Brakespeare.

"Maybe they're going to put some turfs on the mud," said Lily Hanrahan. "Only the turfs haven't come yet either."

"Maybe they've sprinkled some wild-flower seeds on it so that a proper nature garden will grow out of the mud," said Oliver Cornwall.

"I can't see any seeds," I said, peering at the mud really closely.

"I can't see any seeds either," said Gabby, almost touching the mud with her nose.

"Me neither," said Jack Beechwhistle, grabbing a handful of mud and sifting it through his fingers.

"Me neither," said Harry.

"Me neither," said Colin.

No one could see any seeds. No one could see any anything – just little stones, medium stones, big stones and mud.

"I suspect this is an organic nature garden in the truest sense," said Barry Morely.

Barry usually sits on the quiet bench. He is so clever he could present nature programmes on the telly if he wanted to. Or maths programmes, or science programmes, or history programmes – any kind of programme really.

Trouble is, sometimes no one understands what he is saying.

"Come again?" said Jack.

"A truly organic nature garden will take much longer to establish itself," Barry explained. "It needs wind, rain, sunshine and time for seeds to spread and grow."

"We haven't got any seeds." Gabby frowned. "We've only got mud."

"In time, seeds will be carried to our garden in natural ways, like on birds' feet," said Barry. "Or in bird wotsits."

Jack grinned. "He means poop."

"The first meadows, forests and even jungles all grew this way," said Barry.

"How long will a jungle take to grow?" I asked.

"I don't think our nature garden is big enough to ever become a jungle," said Barry.

"How long will a forest take?" I asked.

"The same goes for a forest," said Barry.

"What about a really small meadow?" asked Gabby.

"An extremely small meadow is kind of possible," said Barry, "as long as the right types of seed are transferred."

"How do birds carry seeds on their feet?" asked Daniel McNicholl.

"In their socks," sniggered Jack.

"The seeds of some flowers and bushes have sticky stuff around them," explained Barry. "If a bird treads on the sticky stuff, then the seed gets stuck to its foot. Seeds can be carried for miles by birds' feet."

"Or in birds' bottoms," chuckled Bernadette.

"You mean, to get an even half-decent nature garden, we are going to have to wait for a whole load of birds to walk or poo all over our mud?!" groaned Gabby.

"Kind of," said Barry.

"Hopefully some turfs will arrive tomorrow," I said.

CHAPTER 4

When I told my mum about our new school mud garden, she said, "Organic is all the rage at the moment, Daisy. Organic is the biz!"

"Not in our school it isn't," I said. "In our school, organic takes too long."

The turfs didn't arrive on Tuesday. And they still weren't there when we got to school on Wednesday morning either. Too long had now become even longer!

"You'd think there would be some nature in our nature garden by now," said Daniel Carrington, staring really hard at the mud.

"Like a caterpillar," said Harry.

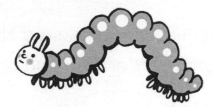

"Or a beetle," said Colin.

"Or a spider," said Melanie.

"I don't like spiders," said Nishta.

"A money spider then," said Melanie.

"I still don't like spiders," said Nishta.

"Even teensy ones."

"A ladybird would be nice," said Fiona Tucker. "Ladybirds are really pretty."

"A wolverine would be even better," said Jack. "Wolverines are the coolest animals on Earth."

"So are wolves," said Harry.

"So are hyenas," said Colin.

"Hold on," said Jack. "They can't ALL be the coolest animal on Earth. Only one of them can."

"I meant second coolest," said Harry.

"I meant third coolest," said Colin.

"Did you know that a hyena has one of the most powerful jaws of any creature in the animal kingdom?" said

 Barry. "The force of a spotted hyena's bite can equate to a thousand pounds of pressure per square inch."

"What's the first most powerful animal bite?" asked Colin.

"Crocodile or alligator," said Barry. "Then hippo, then jaguar, then gorilla, then polar bear, then hyena."

"A wolverine is still the coolest animal on Earth," said Jack, "because you can't train any of the others to do tricks."

"How do you teach wolverines to do tricks?" asked Barry.

"Wolverine whispering," said Jack.

"I wish you could teach some nature to come into our nature garden," said Gabby.

"Yes, Jack," I said. "Do some nature whispering!"

"I THINK I SEE SOME NATURE!" squealed Vicky Carrow, suddenly pointing at the mud.

"It's a feather," said Sanjay, leaning over the brick wall and picking up something really small and white with two fingers.

"We don't want a feather in our nature garden," said Jasmine Smart. "We want the bird that was attached to the feather!"

"Sorry," said Vicky.

"I thought it might be a really small butterfly lying on its side having a sleep."

No one said anything, not even Jack.

After two whole days of waiting, our school nature garden had no caterpillars on it, no beetles on it, no spiders on it, no ladybirds on it, no really small butterflies lying on their sides having a sleep on it, no grass on it, no seeds on it, OR even a bird with sticky feet on it. We hadn't even seen a bird with NON-sticky feet land on it! Or even a FLY with sticky feet land on it! Or even a fly with NORMAL FEET land on it!!!

"Secret meeting at the hopscotch square during morning break!" I whispered as the bell started to ring. "Pass it on."

"Will do," whispered Gabby, turning to Stephanie, who had already started passing it on to everybody else.

By the time we had finished morning register, every single person in our class (except Mrs Peters) knew exactly where they needed to be at break time. And everyone had been warned to bring their secret voices!

The **trouble with secret voices** is, if they are too quiet, no one can hear what you are saying. Even if you've formed a secret circle.

"I can't hear you," whispered Sanjay.

"I can't hear you either," whispered Lottie and Dottie.

"No one can hear you," whispered Jack.

"I SAID, 'IF NATURE WON'T COME TO US, THEN WE NEED TO GO TO NATURE!'" I shouted.

"Too loud!" said Gabby, taking her arm off my shoulder and giving her ears a rub.

"That wasn't a secret voice!" said Nishta, standing up straight and putting her hands over her ears.

Honestly, you try and do something in secret, and everyone else's close-up hearing skills nearly ruin it! Luckily there were no teachers standing nearby when I started shouting. If there had been, my whole entire secret plan would have been ruined!

Once our secret circle had got back into a secret circle again, I told everyone exactly what my plan was.

"Our new school nature garden is the worst school nature garden in—"

"In the universe," interrupted Jack.

"Agreed?" I said.

"Agreed." Everyone nodded.

"A school nature garden should have nature in it, not just mud. And we shouldn't have to wait about a hundred years for the nature to arrive. Agreed?"

"Agreed!" Everyone nodded.

"So let's not wait any longer," I said. "If nature won't come to us, let's go to nature instead!"

"How do you mean?" whispered Gabby.

"I mean, when we get home this

56

afternoon, let's look in our gardens, find some nature and bring it in!"

"To school, you mean?" asked Barry.

"Yes!" I said. "Let's find some nature, bring it to school, and turn our mud garden into a nature garden with actual nature in it!"

It was a genius idea. In fact, it was such a genius idea that everyone in our secret circle didn't just *say* "Agreed", they shouted "AGREED!" so loudly that both teachers in our playground turned around and looked at us!!!!

But it was OK, because the teachers' ears were normal-sized ears, so neither of them had any idea what we had secretly agreed on. Our secret plan was still totally, totally secret!

"I know what I'm going to bring to school," said Jack Beechwhistle as we turned our secret circle into more of a secret square.

"What?" I asked.

"A grizzly bear," he whispered.

"A grizzly bear?!" gasped Paula Potts. "Where are you going to get a grizzly bear from?!"

"That would be telling," Jack said, tapping the side of his nose.

"I'm going to look for butterflies," said Gabby. "I've seen some pretty yellow ones in my garden."

"They'll be brimstones," said Barry. "Male brimstone butterflies, actually. They are the really yellow ones. Brimstones are mostly common to the southern half of England."

"I'll tell you what's mostly common to my garden," said David Alexander. "Slugs. Slugs eat my mum's lettuces all the time."

"Definitely get some slugs," said Jack.

"I'm going to look for ladybirds," said Dottie.

"Seven-spot, five-spot or thirteen-spot?" asked Barry.

"Just ladybirds," she said.

"I'm going to look for manbirds," said Colin with a grin.

"There's no such thing as manbirds," said Harry.

"I know," sighed Colin. "It was a joke."

"Whatever you look for, make sure you can hide it in your school bag," I told everyone. "When we get to school tomorrow morning, we don't want everyone knowing we've brought nature with us."

"Yes, JACK!" said Gabby. "A grizzly bear isn't exactly going to fit inside your school bag, IS IT?!"

"A grizzly bear cub would," he said.

"Not if the mother bear sees you first," said Barry. "An angry grizzly could chase you faster than a greyhound."

"And bite you harder than a hyena," said Colin, remembering what Barry had said earlier.

"If you take a grizzly bear cub from its mother, you won't be putting her cub in your school bag – the mother will be putting *you* in her *mouth*!!"

"Not if I run faster than a greyhound, she won't," said Jack.

"You only came third on Sports Day!" said Gabby.

"That's because I only stayed in third gear," he said.

That's the **trouble with Jack**. He has an answer for absolutely everything.

"Listen, everyone!" I said as the bell began to ring. "Whatever nature we bring in to school tomorrow, we HAVE to keep it a secret. Agreed?"

"AGREED!" everyone shouted in not-very-secret voices at all.

CHAPTER 6

As soon as I got home from school on Wednesday I went straight out into my back garden and looked for some nature.

Actually, no I didn't – I got changed first.

"MUM, WHERE ARE MY GREEN CLOTHES???!" I shouted down the stairs.

"YOU HAVEN'T GOT ANY GREEN CLOTHES!" Mum shouted back.

"*WHY* HAVEN'T I GOT ANY GREEN CLOTHES?" I shouted. "I NEED GREEN CLOTHES!!!!"

"BECAUSE YOU DON'T LIKE GREEN CLOTHES," Mum shouted back. "WHY DO YOU NEED GREEN CLOTHES?"

"SO I CAN BLEND IN WITH NATURE!!!!" I shouted.

That's another **trouble with nature**. You have to wear green clothes or it will see you coming.

"BLEND IN WITH NATURE IN YOUR JEANS AND RED T-SHIRT INSTEAD!" Mum shouted. "ALL YOUR OTHER CLOTHES ARE IN THE WASH!"

The **trouble with blending in with nature in the wrong clothes** is, it can make things really difficult.

When I stepped out into my back garden in my jeans and T-shirt, I did the slooooooooooooooooooooooooowest step that I have ever done in my life. But the blackbird I was after still saw me and flew off straight away. Because I was wearing blue and red.

So I had to look for some different kinds of nature instead.

The **trouble with looking for different kinds of nature instead** is, I'd never looked for *any* kind of nature

before. The only thing I normally do in my back garden is play with Gabby. So in the end I just decided to look everywhere. Starting with the grass.

The **trouble with grass** is, if your mum is too lazy to mow the lawn, it can get really long. Which means that when you kneel down and look in your grass, all you can see is grass.

Even when I pressed my cheek to the grass, all I could see was grass. So I decided to look in some bushes instead.

The **trouble with bushes** is there are only two bushes in my back garden. And both of them have prickles.

So I decided to look in my mum's flowerbeds instead. Looking in my mum's flowerbeds was definitely the right thing to do because, guess what!? As soon as I bent down and looked really closely, I began seeing nature ALL OVER THE PLACE!

I saw three bees
inside three different flowers.

I saw two flies flying around
in ziggerdy-zaggerdy lines
by the wall.

I even saw an actual beetle crawling
over some actual mud with actual legs
and everything!!!!

As soon as I realized that beetles have actual legs and everything, I ran back up to my bedroom and grabbed my magnifying glass. Magnifying glasses are the most totally awesome way to look at every type of nature close up.

Well, they are, and they're not.

The good thing about magnifying glasses is, they let you see nature in real actual close-up!

Did you know that beetles have six legs and really shiny shells!?

Did you know that bumblebees are really fluffy and have funny sticky-up eyebrows!?

Did you know
that butterflies
have even prettier
close-up patterns
on their wings!?

I didn't.

Did you know that ants carry
things above their heads and they

come in two colours – black ones and red ones!?

I didn't!

The **trouble with magnifying glasses** is, they can also show you things you don't want to actually see!

Did you know that beetles have nippers on their faces?

Did you know that bumblebees have stingers on their bottoms?

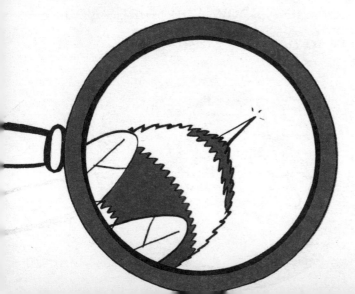

Did you know that butterflies have really creepy legs!

And did you know that black and red ants have real-life actual fights?

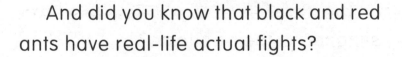

I didn't, but it's a good job I found out. Because the **trouble with stingers** is, they can sting.

The **trouble with legs** is, they can wriggle.

The **trouble with wings** is, they can flutter.

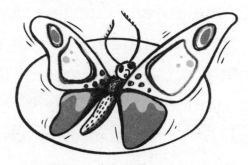

AND FLITTER!!
AND PROBABLY EVEN
FLOTTER!!!!!!!!

As soon as I realized just how nippy and stingy, flittery, flottery and fighty some creepy-crawlies can be, I decided it would be better not to pick any nature up with my actual fingers. Getting your actual fingers creepy-crawled on is one of the creepiest and crawliest things that can ever happen to you. Especially if the nippy, stingy, flittery-flottery-fighty bits are out to get you!!!!!

Luckily my mum had some gardening gloves in the shed.

Well, luckily-ish.

CHAPTER 7

The **trouble with gardening gloves** is, they really need to be the right size. Otherwise your fingers go all floppy.

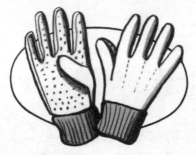

Trouble is, just as I was going to take them off, I saw a spider in the shed window.

The **trouble with seeing a spider in a shed window** is, I'd never seen a spider in a shed window before. Especially through a magnifying glass.

Guess how many legs a spider has in actual magnified close-up?

Not six. EIGHT!

Guess how hairy a spider's legs are in actual magnified close-up?

VERY hairy!!

Guess how hairy a spider's body is?

SUPER hairy!!!!

AND they've got pointy nippers on their face!!!!!

AND they've got furry feelers!!!!!!!

AND they've got bulging black eyes!!!!!!!!!!!!!!!

No wonder Nishta doesn't like spiders.
I bet even spiders don't like spiders!

Trouble is, I knew that if I could get one in my school bag, I would be a total hero in my class. Especially a bulging-eyed, hairy shed spider.

So I worked out a spider-catching plan.

My first plan was to not get too close, hold up my school bag with one gardening glove, and kind of point the spider out of his web and into my school bag with my other gardening glove. Trouble is, spiders don't really understand pointing. Well, bulging-eyed, hairy shed spiders don't.

So I switched to Plan B.

My Plan B was to still not get too close, hold up my school bag as next to the spider as possible without getting too close, and then kind of blow the spider out of his web and into my school bag. Trouble is, when I lifted my school bag in front of my face, I couldn't see where I was blowing.

Plan C was to hold my school bag a bit lower, hold a really shiny silver-coloured garden trowel just above the spider, wait for him to look up and see how ugly his reflection was, then catch him in my school bag when he fell out of his web with fright. Trouble is, I'm not sure spiders look up at garden trowels very much. Not in my shed anyway.

I wish I'd never thought of Plan D.

Plan D was to put my school bag on the floor with the zip wide open, sneak up really sneakily, grab the spider out of his web, drop him into my school bag and do the zip up straight away!

I really, really, really wish I'd never thought of Plan D.

The **trouble with Plan D** is, it gave my mum's gardening gloves the shakes. It was almost as though the gardening gloves were actually scared!

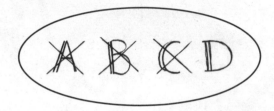

The **trouble with wearing scared gardening gloves** is, anything can happen.

Especially if, just as you get really close to the spider, two of your longest fingers flop into the web without you meaning them to.

The **trouble with flopping scared gardening-glove fingers into a web** is, it suddenly made the spider run!

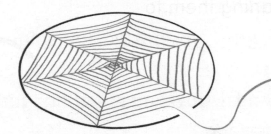

Honestly, if you think a cheetah can run fast with four legs, imagine how fast a spider can run with eight! I mean, one minute he was in the web, the next second he was running down the wall.

Then across the floor.

And right across my shoes!

I nearly had a heart attack!

I nearly had an eyebrow attack!!

I definitely had a floppy-fingers attack!!!!

I gave up looking for spiders after that.

And I gave up wearing gardening gloves too.

CHAPTER 8

The **trouble with giving up wearing gardening gloves** is, it only left me with a magnifying glass, a school bag and bare fingers – which is right back where I started.

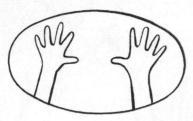

So I decided to switch to twigs.

The brilliant thing about twigs is, you can get right up close to nature without your fingers doing any of the touching.

Because all you have to hold with your fingers is the twig, not the nature!

The **trouble with twigs** though is, sometimes the ones in my garden get the shakes too!

The first twig I tried looked perfect. It was brown, slightly knobbly, really thin and about twenty centimetres long. If I was a beetle, I would definitely have wanted to crawl straight up my twig and all the way into my school bag. Trouble is, the beetles in my garden didn't want to crawl up my shaky twig at all. They just wanted to crawl over it, under it, round it and past it!

Even when I poked the twig right in their faces, they didn't want to crawl up it.

So I gave up looking for beetles.

The second twig I tried was even better, because it was much longer and it still had some green leaves and a piece of purple flower attached.

I thought that when I held out my second twig, bees and butterflies would land all over it. But they didn't. Even when I pressed the end of my second twig right into the middle of some flower petals, they didn't even bother to sniff my purple flower!

So I gave up looking for bees and butterflies too.

The **trouble with giving up on bees, butterflies and beetles (not forgetting spiders)** is, it makes you realize that whatever nature you find in your back garden, it doesn't want to go inside school bags. It wants to go inside flower petals and down tiny holes or under rocks instead. At least the nature in my back garden does.

The more places I poked my twigs into, the more nature I kept finding. I discovered types of nature I'd never even seen before! There was a long black beetly thing under a brick near the fence. There were some shorter, brown creepy-crawly things with nippers on their faces under the watering can. I even found a centipede under our barbecue-charcoal bag! (Everyone knows what a centipede looks like, even if you've never seen a centipede before.)

It still didn't want to go into my school bag though.

So I tried to catch Tiptoes instead.

The **trouble with catching Tiptoes** is, he's not my own actual cat.

He belongs to my neighbour, Mrs Pike. If Tiptoes had been my own actual cat, I could have put him in my school bag just like that. Because I would have been the boss.

If you ask me, Tiptoes would be the perfect kind of animal to put in a school nature garden. He's a really lovely gingery colour, he's got nice whiskers, a fluffy coat, he can purr when he wants to and he doesn't have a stinger on his bottom.

Trouble is, I've tried catching him before. Not to put him in my school bag or anything – just to stroke him, and play games with him, and teach him how to speak human.

I guess Tiptoes isn't the kind of cat who likes being stroked, or playing tea parties, or learning new languages. He just wants to be left alone.

Well, left alone by me anyway.

Even when I made a milk trail all the way across the lawn and up to the ham I'd put in my school bag, he STILL stayed on the wall.

So I gave up trying to catch Tiptoes as well.

As far as I could see, there wasn't a single piece of nature in my garden that wanted to go in my school bag all by itself. Even after I'd taken the ham out of my school bag and swapped it for some Mini Cheddars.

I thought nature would love Mini Cheddars. I was sure that if I put my bag on the lawn with five Mini Cheddars in it, left it for about two minutes and then looked inside, I'd have at least two mice and a yellow butterfly (because mice love cheese, and yellow butterflies are the same colour as Mini Cheddars).

But I didn't. All I still had inside my school bag was the five Mini Cheddars.

By the time I'd eaten them, I had completely run out of ideas. My *first* ever nature hunt had turned into my *worst* ever nature hunt! I'd been round my whole entire garden about six times, with gardening gloves and twigs and ham and milk and a magnifying glass and everything, and STILL my school bag was completely empty.

What were my friends going to say when I went to school the next day with an empty school bag? It wouldn't have been so bad if it hadn't been MY IDEA to get nature in our school bags and take it to school in the actual first place! The last person everyone would be expecting to have NO nature in their school bag was me!

If I didn't get some nature in my school bag fast, the next day at school was going to be the most embarrassing day of my entire life.

I'd have to do loads of explaining.

I'd have to do loads of apologizing.

In fact, I'd probably have to change schools.

Thank goodness I remembered to put away Mum's gardening gloves!

CHAPTER 9

When I called for Gabby on Thursday morning, I was so excited I could have burst.

"Have you found any nature?" I said the moment she opened her front door.

"Yes," said Gabby. "Have you?"

"YES!" I said, tapping my school bag. "And I've taught it to do tricks!"

"TRICKS???!!!" she gasped.

"Actual tricks!" I nodded.

As soon as Gabby found out that the nature I had in my school bag did actual tricks, she wanted me to show it to her straight away. But I wouldn't. Because it was a secret. PLUS my mum might have seen me take it out of my bag. PLUS it might have escaped. PLUS I really, really wanted to wait till we got to school.

"Pleeeeeeease tell me what kind of nature you've found!" pleaded Gabby as we set off down the road.

"I can't," I giggled.

"Please, please, please tell me," she begged.

"I can't, I can't, I can't," I laughed.

"Why, why, why?" she whined.

"Because I don't know what kind of nature it is!" I chuckled. "I've never seen any nature like it before. All I know is, the moment I touched it, it started doing tricks!"

"What kind of tricks?" Gabby asked.

"Wait till we get to school and I'll show you!" I told her.

"Give me a clue!" she begged.

"No," I said.

"I'll be your best friend," she promised.

"You're already my best friend!" I said.

"All right then – if you don't tell me, I *won't* be your best friend," she said.

"You'll *always* be my best friend," I laughed. "And anyway, never mind about my nature, what kind of nature have *you* found?"

"Two worms and a caterpillar!" she blurted.

That's the **trouble with Gabby**. She couldn't keep a secret if she tried.

It was a brilliant start to my secret plan though. We hadn't even got to school yet, and already we had two worms, a caterpillar, and something else I didn't know the name of to put in our school nature garden.

"I knew we'd both be brilliant at finding nature," I said. "I never even thought of looking for a worm!"

"I like my caterpillar best," said Gabby. "I found her eating stinging nettles at the end of my garden. She doesn't do tricks though."

"Stinging nettles!!!" I shuddered. "I'm not actually sure what my nature eats . . . There weren't any leaves where I found it. Only dirt and dampish dust."

"Where *did* you find it?" asked Gabby. "If you tell me where you found it, I might be able to look for one in my garden as well!"

"It was underneath my mum's seed trays," I told her. "I was just putting her gardening gloves back in the shed when I saw the seed trays and thought:

Mmmm, Daisy, you've looked for nature under rocks and you've looked for nature under the watering can and you've looked under some bricks and you've looked under a barbecue-charcoal bag, but you haven't looked under some seed trays . . . So I did! And – bingo! There it was!"

"There *what* was?" said Gabby, trying to trick me into telling her something I'd already said I didn't know the answer to.

"I've told you – I don't know what it is!" I said.

"Has it got wings?" she asked.

"Wait and see," I said.

"Has it got legs?" she asked.

"Might have. Might not have!" I told her. "I'm still not telling you or showing you till we get to school or it will spoil the surprise!"

"I hate you," Gabby fibbed.

"No you don't!" I laughed.

"Yes I do," she laughed back.

"No you don't."

"Yes I do."

"No you don't."

"Yes I do."

"No you don't."

"Yes I do."

Thank goodness it wasn't very far to school.

CHAPTER 10

When Gabby and I walked through the school gates, we knew straight away that my secret plan had worked. Jack Beechwhistle was standing by the nature garden, Harry and Colin were standing by the nature garden – so was Paula, so was Lottie, so was Dottie, so was Barry, so was Nishta. EVERYONE was standing by the nature garden, and everyone had actual nature in their school bags to secretly show and tell!

"I've got a beetle!" said Harry.

"I've got a ladybird!" said Sanjay.

"I've got a slug!" said Daniel.

"I've got *three* slugs!" said Liberty Pearce.

"I've got a slug with a crash helmet on!" said Paula Potts.

"That's a snail!" sighed Barry.

"I've got five greenflies," said Richard Stokes.

"I've got some grass cuttings!" said Asif.

"I've got my mum's favourite pot plant!" said Vicky.

"I found it on the window ledge in our lounge!"

119

"I've got a caterpillar that can live on the leaves!" said Bernadette.

"Me too!" said Jasmine.

"Me too!" said Fiona.

The only people who hadn't been able to bring any nature to school were:

Liam (his mum had found their pet parrot in his school bag).
Lily (she'd got stung trying to pick up a wasp).
Chelsea (she'd fallen into her fishpond trying to look for frogs).
And Oliver (he'd broken a vase trying to catch a fly with his hands).

Apart from that, we had nature all over the place! Well, we would have once we'd taken it out of our school bags and put it on our mud.

"OK, we've only got fifteen minutes before the bell. I'm going to get my secret nature out last," I whispered, with a wink at Gabby. "Who wants to go first?"

"I will," she whispered back, unzipping her school bag and taking out two yoghurt pots with breathe-through paper taped to the top.

"Me next," said Harry.

"Me next," said Colin.

"Me next," said Paula.

One by one, whisper by whisper, we emptied our secret nature onto the mud. None of the teachers saw what we were doing. None of the teachers even suspected!

"Run wild," whispered Stephanie, tipping a ladybird out of an envelope.

"Run free," whispered David, eventually managing to shake two slugs out of a Tupperware pot.

"Be happy," whispered Harry to his beetle.

"Catch some teachers in your web and suck their brains out," said Jack Beechwhistle, taking a spider out of his pocket with his bare hands and dropping it on the mud.

"I thought you were bringing in a grizzly bear?" Paula frowned.

"It got confiscated," Jack said with a shrug.

I told you – Jack has an answer for everything. Even missing grizzly bears.

By the time everyone had emptied their envelopes, yoghurt pots, jam jars, Tupperware pots, tins, plastic bags, pencil cases and matchboxes, I had counted:

1 spider
11 worms
6 snails
6 slugs
5 ants
2 beetles
1 grasshopper
3 ladybirds

6 caterpillars

12 greenflies

1 pot plant

Some grass cuttings, and

1 dead moth (don't worry, the moth
was dead when
Nishta found it!)

I also found out from Barry that long
brown creepy-crawlies with nippers

on their faces are called
earwigs. And the big
black beetly thing I'd
seen under my barbecue-
charcoal bag was a Devil's coach
horse! Gulp!

Gabby didn't do any counting. All she could think about was the nature I had hidden in my school bag and what tricks it was going to do.

"Daisy's taught her secret nature to do tricks!" she blurted, unable to keep my secret secret any longer.

"TRICKS!!!!" everyone gasped.

"ACTUAL tricks!" I nodded.

CHAPTER 11

The **trouble with secret nature that does actual tricks** is, everyone wanted to see it straight away. Which I suppose was a good job really, because we only had about three minutes before morning lessons started.

"Gather round quickly, everyone," I said, unzipping the zip on my school bag.

"Not too close," I said as I took my empty Mini Cheddars packet out of my bag.

Everyone was so excited to see my secret nature, they completely forgot about not getting too close.

"Get ready to be amazed," I said, tipping up my Mini Cheddars packet and rolling my secret nature into the palm of my actual hand.

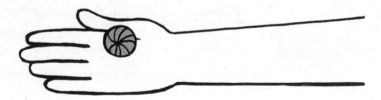

Yes, I know, my ACTUAL HAND! I actually had some actual secret nature in my ACTUAL HAND! I'll tell you about that later.

"It looks like a grey pea!" said Paula.

"Uncurl!" I said, waving my fingers like a wizard and then holding up my secret nature for everyone to see.

"It's uncurling!" gasped Gabby. "It's turning into a grey pea with legs!"

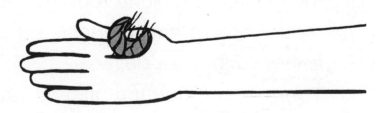

She was right: instead of being curled up like a ball, my secret nature was now beginning to open up and wriggle!

"FOURTEEN LEGS!" I grinned. "I've counted them!"

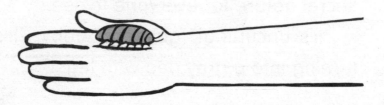

The moment everyone realized that my secret nature had fourteen secret legs, they came even closer.

"Hey presto! Curl up into a ball

again!" I said, tapping my secret nature on the back with my finger.

"It's curling up into a ball again!" gasped Gabby. "Now it looks like a grey pea *without* legs!"

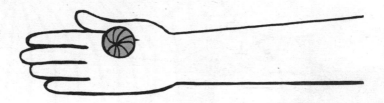

"I told you it could do tricks!" I smiled.

"They're not tricks," said Barry, squeezing through to the front for the closest look out of anyone. "It's a defence mechanism."

"And it's not a grey pea with legs either," said Jack. "It's a woodlouse."

"Jack's right, Daisy," said Barry. "It's a common woodlouse."

As soon as everyone heard I'd brought an actual woodlouse to school, they moved in even closer!

"If it's so common, how come no one else has brought one?" I said, realizing that Barry and Jack were a little bit jealous.

"I thought everyone was going to bring woodlices in," said Jack, "so I didn't even bother."

"Does it do anything else?" asked Gabby, not really caring whether it was a trick or a defence mechanism.

"Watch this!" I tilted the palm of my hand like a slide and pointed my fingers at the mud. "HEY PRESTO – ROLLLLLLL!!!!"

The moment I tilted my hand, my secret nature did exactly as I had commanded, rollllllllllllllllllllling just like a ball, all the way across my palm, down my fingers and straight onto the mud!

"Do all woodlouses do tricks?" asked Gabby, giving my secret nature the loudest clap she could without the teachers being able to hear.

"All woodlice have defence mechanisms, if that's what you mean,"

138

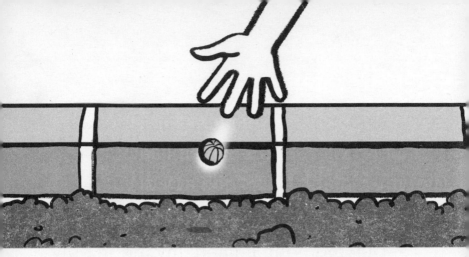

said Barry. "Their articulated body armour allows them to curl up into a ball the instant they feel threatened."

"I wasn't threatening him." I frowned. "I was giving him magic commands."

"Rolling up into a ball is still a defence mechanism, not magic," said Jack.

"Well, it looks like magic to me," said Gabby.

"And me," I said as the bell rang.

"And me!"

"And me!"

"And me!"

"And me!"

"And me!"

"And me!"

"And me!" said just about everybody who'd never seen a woodlouse before either.

There was absolutely no doubt about it. Of all the secret nature people had brought in, mine was totally the best.

"As soon as morning lessons are over, let's come back and see how our nature has settled in!" said Gabby as we headed into class for morning register.

"Good idea." I nodded, dropping my Mini Cheddars packet into a bin along the way. "And if Mrs Peters asks us to do any work at all during morning lessons, let's tell her we're not doing any school stuff today, we're just going to think up new tricks for my woodlouse!"

"Maybe NOT such a good idea," chuckled Gabby.

CHAPTE

When the bell for morni[ng]
we ran out of class so fas[t]
we didn't get arrested.

"Last one to the nature g[arden]
earwig!" said Paula Potts.

"YOU'RE AN EARWIG, LILY!" everyone
shouted as Lily Hanrahan tripped over
her shoelaces by the quiet bench.

That's the **trouble with shoelaces**.
They're not Velcro.

"That's not fair!" Lily shouted, rubbing her knee, racing over to the nature garden and slapping her fingertips onto the brick wall.

"You're still an earwig," said Paula.

The **trouble with Lily being an earwig** is, after about thirty seconds of looking at our nature garden we realized she was the only earwig we had left.

Because Melanie Simpson's earwig had completely vanished.

"Where's all our nature gone?" said Gabby, searching the mud with her fingers to see where her caterpillar and worms had gone.

"Where's my ladybird?" said Sanjay.

"My worms aren't here!" said Gabby.

"Or mine," said Lottie.

"Or mine," said Dottie.

"Where's my beetle?" said Harry.

"And my grass cuttings?" said Asif.

No one could believe their eyeballs. In the space of just two morning lessons, everyone's secret nature HAD COMPLETELY VANISHED!

Even worse, my woodlouse had vanished with them!!!

"Where's our nature gone?" groaned Dottie.

"Maybe they've been kidnapped by another school with a nature garden that's even worse than ours," said Vicky Carrow.

"Or maybe they've been eaten," said Jack Beechwhistle. "Maybe, while Mrs Peters was forcing us to learn our times tables, a flock of hungry thrushes and blackbirds swooped down and ate everything in sight."

"Don't say that!" I gasped. "I loved my woodlouse!"

"I loved my caterpillar too!" said Gabby.

"Not as much as hungry blackbirds and thrushes would have loved them." Jack frowned. "I bet my spider was the first to get gobbled up."

"I'm afraid Jack could be right," said Barry. "Although introducing some home-grown nature into our school nature garden seemed like a good idea, the absence of ground cover could have left our nature rather exposed to predatory birds."

"What did he just say?" I whispered to Gabby.

"He said our secret nature had nowhere to hide from hungry blackbirds and thrushes," she explained.

"Or seagulls,"
said Jack.
"Or eagles
or buzzards
or sparrow hawks
or kestrels
or snowy owls."

"All right, don't go on!" I said with a stamp of my foot. "And anyway, our worms *do* have somewhere to hide. They've got a whole load of mud to hide in!"

"Daisy's right!" said Sanjay. "Maybe our worms have burrowed out of sight."

"And maybe the rest of our secret nature has followed the worms down their holes!" said Nishta.

"Could a ladybird squeeze down a wormhole, Barry?" asked Bernadette.

"I guess so," said Barry. "If the hole was big enough."

"So could greenflies then," said Richard.

"And a spider, if it tucked its legs in," said Jack.

"That's definitely what must have happened," said Gabby. "Instead of all our secret nature living on top of our mud like we thought it was going to, it is now living deep down inside our mud instead!"

"Our nature is living happily ever under," Jasmine said with a smile.

"How did the snails crawl down the wormholes?" asked Harry. "Snail shells are far too big to get down wormholes."

"The snails must have crawled off somewhere else," said Colin.

"Or taken their shells off and

changed into slugs," said Paula.

"The most important thing is, they haven't been eaten by thrushes or blackbirds," I said, much preferring Sanjay's version of what had happened to Jack Beechwhistle's. "Our secret nature is safe and sound living deep underground. The only problem is, we can't see it."

"Which means all of our hard work was for nothing," sighed Nishta as the bell rang again.

"We could just as well have left our secret nature in our back gardens and let normal nature come on its own, like Mr Copford said it would," said Gabby as we went back to our classroom.

"Or maybe we should have found some nature that doesn't have to hide from hungry birds down wormholes."

"How do you mean?" asked Gabby.

"I mean, Gabby," I said, lowering my voice to a whisper so whispery even I could barely hear it, "if we want to have a half-decent school nature garden that doesn't take a trillion years to arrive, it's time for you and me to think BIG!"

CHAPTER 13

"What about a horse?" said Gabby as we walked home after school on Thursday afternoon.

"If we can find a horse tonight, we can borrow some sugar lumps from somewhere and get it to follow us to school tomorrow morning!"

"We'd never be able to lift a horse up onto the mud," I said.

"What about a sheep?" she said.

"No, a goat!" I said. "If we found a mountain goat, it could jump up onto the mud all by itself!"

"Sheep and goats live on grass, not mud," said Gabby.

"Pigs like mud! In fact, pigs LOVE mud!!" I said. "If we can get a pig from

somewhere, we'd have the best school nature garden in the world!"

"If we get *two* pigs, we can have piglets!" said Gabby.

"But not bacon, though." I frowned. "We're definitely not letting Mr Copford use our nature garden for his sandwiches."

"Or school dinners," added Gabby. "Where are we going to get a pig from though?"

That's the **trouble with living where Gabby and I live**. The only biggish animals you get are cats and dogs. And they already live somewhere else.

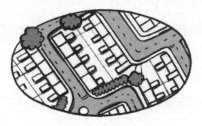

"Are you sure your cat wouldn't want to come and live on our school nature garden instead?" I asked.

"Pretty sure," said Gabby. "And anyway, I'd miss him when I wasn't at school."

"You don't think he could catch us a mouse, do you?" I asked.

"Not without killing it," said Gabby. "Do you miss your woodlouse?"

"Kind of," I said. "I only had half a day to get to know him."

"I'm surprised you picked him up with your bare hands," said Gabby. "I didn't think you liked doing things like that."

"I pick peas off my dinner plate all

the time." I shrugged. "The first time he rolled into a ball, I just imagined he was a pea instead of a creepy-crawly."

"That's really funny," chuckled Gabby. "Why do you think he's called a woodlouse?"

"Because if I ever asked him to do a trick, he WOOD!" I laughed. "WOOD/ WOULD – get it?"

"Yes, I get it!" Gabby smiled. "Was the seed tray you found him under made of wood?" she asked.

"Yes," I said.

"Was the seed tray on top of that wooden seed tray made of wood?" she asked.

"Yes, why?" I asked.

"And were the seed trays on top of those wooden seed trays made of wood too?" she asked.

"Yes – but tell me why you keep asking?" I asked.

"Because your woodlouse might have given me a BIG idea!" Gabby grinned.

"How big?"

"BIG BIG!"

"HOW BIG BIG?"

"BIG BIG BIG!!!"

"Tell me what it is," I said.

"Not until I've spoken to my dad," Gabby told me.

"Spoken to your dad about *what*?" I asked, trying to trick her into telling me something she didn't want to tell me.

"Wait and see," she said.

"I'll be your best friend," I promised.

"You're already my best friend!" she pointed out.

"All right then – if you don't tell me, I *won't* be your best friend," I said.

"You'll *always* be my best friend," she said. "And anyway, when you had a secret this morning you wouldn't tell me yours!"

"I hate you," I fibbed.

"No you don't!" she laughed.

"Yes I do," I laughed back.

"No you don't."

"Yes I do."

"No you don't."

"Yes I do."

"No you don't."

"Yes I do."

"No you don't."

"Yes I do."

What a lonnnnnnnnnnnnnnnnnnnnng wait it was until Friday morning!!!!!!

CHAPTER 14

"CAMPING!" I gasped when I met Gabby for school on Friday morning. "YOUR DAD IS GOING TO TAKE US ACTUAL CAMPING?!!!!"

"Tomorrow! In the woods!" Gabby grinned. "*If* your mum says it's OK!"

"Mum, Mum, Mum," I squealed, running back to my house. "Is it all right if I go camping with Gabby and her dad tomorrow, IN THE ACTUAL WOODS?"

"What a lovely idea," she said. "I can have a girlie night in with Mrs Pike!"

"You can have a girlie night in, and I can have a girlie night out camping!" I whooped, skipping back down the path and giving Gabby the biggest hug ever!

"It was your WOODlouse that gave me the idea of going to the WOODS!" she said.

"Imagine the nature we'll be able to find in the actual woods," I said. "We'll be able to find badgers and foxes and rabbits and . . . and . . . What else will we be able to find?" I frowned.

"We'll ask Barry when we get to school," Gabby said.

"How did I forget squirrels!?!" I squeaked when we met up with Barry by the quiet bench. "Squirrels are some of the woodiest creatures you can get!!!"

"You're more likely to see grey squirrels than red ones," said Barry, "unless you're camping in Scotland."

"Are we camping in Scotland?" I asked Gabby.

"No, we're camping in Potts Wood," she said.

"Definitely grey squirrels then," said Barry. "Look out for deer too – muntjac deer probably. Roe deer if you're lucky. And frogs, if there's a pond, or maybe even a toad. There could be stoats,

there could be weasels and moles and hedgehogs and bats and woodpeckers, and maybe even an adder!!!"

"What's an adder?" I asked.

"It's a poisonous snake," said Jack Beechwhistle, completely butting in where he wasn't wanted. "Adders go hisssssssssssssssssssssssssssssssssss sssssssssssssssssssssssssssssssssssss sssssss," he told us. "Especially in the night when they're trying to crawl into your sleeping bag."

"Ignore him," said Gabby, hooking her arm through mine and pulling me away from the most annoying boy on Earth. "There are no adders in Potts

Wood, and even if there were, we'll have zips on our tent to keep them out."

"Hisssssssssssssssssssssssssssssssss ssssssssssssssssssssssssssssssssssssssss sssss," went Jack again, right in my ear, as we walked into our classroom.

"He's such a boy," I whispered to Gabby as the morning register began.

"He's just jealous that we're going camping and he's not," she whispered back.

"You're right." I smiled. "We're going camping and he's NOT!"

By the end of the register, I had completely forgotten about adders. And Jack Beechwhistle. And lessons.

That's the **trouble with camping** – once you know you're going camping, camping is all you can think about.

Especially if you've never been camping before in your whole entire actual life!

What's camping like? I wrote on a secret note during Literacy.

(I know I shouldn't have, but I did.)

I'll tell you later, Gabby wrote me back on a secret note of her own.

What will I need to take? I wrote on a secret note during our spelling test.

I'll tell you later, she said, giving me the same secret note back.

What will we eat? I asked on a new secret note during History.

I'll tell you later, she said, on the exact same secret note.

That's the **trouble with Gabby's secret notes**. Sometimes she only uses one piece of paper.

It didn't matter though, because by the end of Friday morning break I knew everything I needed to know about camping. Gabby had told me about tents and tent pegs and guy ropes and sleeping bags and cool boxes and camping stoves and zips.

By the end of lunch break we had

decided exactly what clothes we were going to wear, what I was going to pack in my lunch box, how much drink I was going to take, and which pocket I was going to put my three-colour torch in.

By the time school was over, Gabby and I had even agreed exactly what types of nature we wanted to catch in Potts Wood, whereabouts on our school nature garden they were going to live, AND what all the woodland animals we caught were going to be called!

All we had to do now was make our traps!

CHAPTER 15

The **trouble with traps** is they have to be kind ones, especially animal traps. Otherwise they might hurt the animals you are going to be catching.

On the way home from school on Friday, Gabby told me that before her mum and dad bought her cat, they used to catch the mice in their shed with actual mousetraps.

The **trouble with actual mousetraps** is, they don't just *catch* mice, they *squish* them. At least the ones with springs and metal bits on them do.

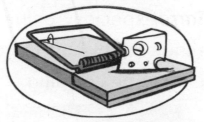

So Gabby and I decided that our traps were going to be totally squish-free.

If your school nature garden is as bad as ours and you need to catch some woodland creatures to make it better, this is how to make homemade squish-free animal traps.

(P.S. Make sure you get your baits when your mum isn't looking.)

Rabbit trap
Bait: Carrot

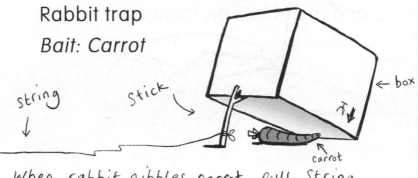

string ↓

stick →

← box

carrot

When rabbit nibbles carrot, pull string

Fox trap
Bait: Chicken nugget

when fox gobbles chicken nugget, pull string

Squirrel trap
Bait: Dry-roasted peanuts

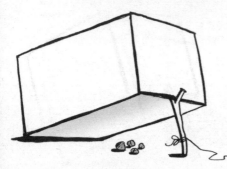

When squirrel munches peanuts, pull string

Badger trap
Bait: Large potato

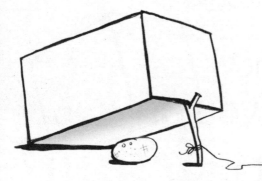

when badger bites potato, pull string

Woodpecker trap
Bait: Wooden spoon

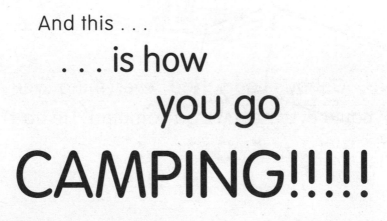

when woodpecker pecks wooden spoon, pull string

And this . . .
. . . is how
you go
CAMPING!!!!!

CHAPTER 16

The **trouble with going camping** is, it's really important that you go with an expert. Not just any old expert either. Someone with at least two tents, three sleeping bags and a cool box on wheels.

Gabby's dad had everything you could ever need to go camping. He had hot-gel hand warmers (even though it was summer), a camping stove, self-inflating sleeping mats, a foldout toaster, lights to hang up inside our tent, lights to hang up outside our tent, pillows for sleeping on, three special camping chairs with cup holes in the arms, a foot pump for blowing up the big tent, spray that mosquitoes don't like, candles that mosquitoes don't like, a mosquito swatter that mosquitoes don't like, and even a Swiss army knife with about forty-two different camping actions. Including a pointy bit for taking stones out of horses' hooves! How expert camping is that!

"Isn't your mum coming with us?" I asked Gabby when her dad had finished loading the car on Saturday morning.

"My mum doesn't like camping," she said, "but she likes it when my dad goes."

"Bye, Daisy!" Mum waved as we pulled off Gabby's drive in the car.

"Bye, sweetie! Bye, honey!" Gabby's mum waved as we set off down the road.

Not going camping in Scotland was actually a really good idea, because according to Gabby's dad it would have taken us about eight hours to get there.

That's the **trouble with red squirrels**. They live in far-too-far-away places.

"How long will it take us to get to Potts Wood?" I asked.

"Only about twenty minutes!" said Gabby.

"There it is!" I cheered, nineteen minutes and twenty-seven seconds later, according to Gabby's watch. "Look at the trees! Look at the grass! Look at the litter bin!"

"And the bushes and the blossom and the flowers!" said Gabby. "There's nature all over the place!"

"There's bound to be squirrels living here." I grinned, undoing my seat belt as soon as Gabby's dad had turned off the car. "There's bound to be absolutely EVERY type of nature living in THIS wood!"

"All we've got to do is catch some of it," added Gabby.

As soon as we had jumped out of the car, me and Gabby helped her dad unload all the camping equipment. Well, we carried the things that were ours.

"Once we've set up camp, we'll go hunting," whispered Gabby, leading the way into the woods.

Potts Wood had leaves and grass all over the place.

And surprises.

"LOOK AT THOSE!" I gasped, pointing to a massive pile of teensy twigs at the bottom of a tree trunk. "THEY'RE HUGE!"

As soon as Gabby saw what I was pointing at, she put her traps down on the grass and bent for a closer look.

"They're wood ants," said her dad, catching us up with his cool box on wheels. "There could be thousands of wood ants in that nest. Millions, even."

The **trouble with wood ants** is, I'd never seen wood ants before. Or even a normal ants' nest.

Wood ants are amazing! And absolutely enormous! In fact, they are so absolutely enormous, you don't even need a magnifying glass to see their faces!

"I bet wood ants don't hide from hungry birds!" I said. "I bet wood ants don't hide from ANYTHING!"

"Even Barry Morely didn't think of wood ants!" said Gabby. "Maybe he's never heard of them!"

"Imagine if we've discovered some nature that even Barry Morely doesn't know about!" I said.

"Or Jack Beechwhistle." Gabby grinned. "He'll be even more jealous of us now!"

"He'll turn greener than a leaf!" I giggled.

"We'll camp in the clearing at the bottom of this track," said Gabby's dad, heading off ahead down the path.

"He's really strong, your dad, isn't he?" I said as we tried to catch up.

"He does press-ups in his bedroom," said Gabby. "And he eats granola."

Potts Wood had everything you could ever want if you were going camping in the woods. In fact, once Gabby's dad had come back from the car for the third time, it even had a portable loo with pink flushy stuff in it!

"No need to wee in the bushes, girls!" he said. "Just use and flush!"

"I'd never even thought about going to the loo in the woods!" I whispered.

"My dad thinks of everything," Gabby whispered back. "Wait till you see our blow-up tent!"

CHAPTER 17

The **trouble with blow-up tents** is, I'd never actually heard of a blow-up tent before. All I'd ever heard of was a put-up tent.

But when I saw how a blow-up tent actually works, I was blown away!

"Stopwatch at the ready, Gabby?" said Gabby's dad, puffing out his cheeks and getting ready to take everything out of the bag.

"Ready . . ." said Gabby. "Steady . . . GO!"

The moment Gabby said "GO", her dad opened the bag and started pulling out all the blow-up tent bits. There was a massive great main tent bit, twelve tent pegs, twelve guy ropes and a foot pump too.

To start off with, the main tent bit looked like it was never going to go up, even after Gabby's dad had spread it out right across the ground and banged tent pegs into the middle edges and all four corners. It was when he undid a plastic screwy bit and fixed his foot pump to the hole that things really started to happen.

Thirteen pumps, and one end of the tent was up!

Thirteen more pumps in another hole, and the middle of the tent was up!

Fifteen more pumps, and a quick drink of water, and the other end of the tent was up too!

It was amazing! In no time at all, a whole entire tent for two people had blown up like a bouncy castle right before our eyes! Inside, it had a bedroom bit at the back for sleeping in and a lounge bit at the front for sitting and talking in. It had see-through plastic windows and really cool zip-up curtains. Even better, Gabby and I would be camping in it on our own! All by ourselves! Together!!!

Even better than even better – it was GREEN!!!!

"Seven minutes and thirty-three seconds!" said Gabby, stopping the stopwatch as the very last guy rope got tightened really tight.

"A new world record!" her dad cheered, raising his arms and then reaching for another drink of water to celebrate.

"This is how you conquer the wilderness, girls! Just watch and learn!"

"GO!" said Gabby's dad, tossing the water bottle onto a chair and starting on the smaller tent straight away.

"I'm glad we're staying in the big tent," I whispered as a second bendy pole got threaded through the inner bit of grey roof cover and then clipped into place. "There's far more room in the big tent. Plus the smaller tent is orange."

"My dad doesn't mind where he sleeps," whispered Gabby as the top bit of the roof cover went over the under bit of the roof cover and then got tied to the tent in three places. "He'd sleep up a tree if he could."

"Only three more tent pegs to go," puffed Gabby's dad, wiping the sweat off his forehead.

"Two minutes and forty-seven

seconds and counting," said Gabby, looking at her watch.

"POOPYPANTS! I mean fiddlesticks!" said her dad, suddenly dropping to his knees and giving a tent peg a tug with both hands.

That's the **trouble with tent pegs**. If you hit them too hard, they can bend.

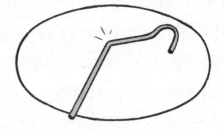

"Three minutes and one second," said Gabby, stopping the stopwatch with her thumb as the last of the six tent pegs got banged into the ground without bending.

"Fiddlesticks again," sighed her dad. "If I hadn't bent that tent peg, I'd have had a double world record."

"You still did really well," said Gabby, giving the stopwatch back to him. "Can Daisy and I go and play in the woods now?" she asked, saying exactly what I was thinking.

"Of course you can," said her dad. "Go and explore, but don't stray too far, and remember to take your emergency whistles."

"Emergency whistles!" I gasped.

"Emergency whistles!" Gabby grinned.

CHAPTER 18

The **trouble with emergency whistles** is, the moment you put one around your neck, it makes you want to blow it even when there isn't an emergency.

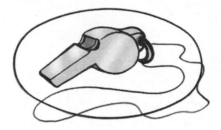

"What kind of emergency do you think we need to have before we can blow our whistles?" I asked Gabby as we went off to explore the woods.

"If we get chased by grizzly bears, we can definitely blow our whistles!" she giggled.

"Or lions!" I laughed.

"Or rhinoceroses or tigers or leopards," Gabby chuckled.

"Bagsy I blow mine first," I said.

"That's not fair," said Gabby.

"OK, bagsy we blow our whistles at exactly the same time!" I said.

Trouble is, there weren't any grizzly bears or lions or tigers in Potts Wood. So we just had to not blow our whistles and have fun instead!

We looked for animals in the woods . . .

We're going on a rabbit hunt!
We're going on a rabbit hunt!

We're going on a squirrel hunt!
We're going on a squirrel hunt!

We're going on a badger hunt!
We're going on a badger hunt!

We're going on a foxy hunt!
We're going on a foxy hunt!

And waited and
waited and waited.

Until nothing came along.

We built a den out of leaves and branches.

We looked for birds . . .

We're going on an ostrich hunt!
We're going on an ostrich hunt!

We looked for the biggest animal we could think of . . .

We're going on a dinosaur hunt!
We're going on a dinosaur hunt!

We looked for salmon and trout in the stream.

And cod.

We had a picnic all by ourselves on our own.

By the time we got back to our tent, it had almost started to nearly start getting dark!

CHAPTER 19

Being back at the tent was just as much fun as looking for nature in the woods. I never realized that there were so many different things you can do when you go camping!

As soon as we had put our empty lunch boxes back into our school bags and zipped up our tent, Gabby and I sat down next to her dad and had two hot dogs with tomato sauce (because we were still hungry after our picnic). Then we had three doughnuts each too (because the jam inside the doughnuts was really jammy), then we tried our drinks holders out two times in a row (because jammy jam and tomatoey tomato sauce makes you really thirsty). Then we listened to stories about being an olden-days child. (Gabby's dad is nearly forty! And he tells good stories!) Then we took it in turns to whittle sticks with Gabby's dad's penknife (because when you're camping, sticks look much better when they have a pointy end). Then we lit an actual camp-fire made with actual twigs, actual logs and extra-long matches. Then we toasted marshmallows on non-shaky sticks, then we lit our special candles (because we didn't want the mosquitoes to nibble us in the dark), then we put some spray on (in case the candles didn't work), then we did Ninja swatting practice (in case the mosquitoes had superpowers against special candles and spray), and after that we sang a camping song called

"Ging Gang Goolie", then a football song called "Ging Gang Goalie", then a boys-not-included song called "Ging Gang Girlie", then we all lay down on a picnic blanket together and looked up at the stars!

Honestly, if you've never laid on your back and looked up at the stars before, you really should. There's millions of them!!!! And there's spaceships with red flashing lights. (Gabby's dad said they were aeroplanes, but I promise you they weren't.)

By the time it was time for actual bed, the only thing Gabby and I hadn't managed to do on our camping trip was catch some actual nature!

And turn the light in our tent off.

The **trouble with turning the light in your tent off** is, it makes your tent go really dark. Especially if it's really dark outside your tent too.

"Let's leave our light on until my dad makes us turn it off," said Gabby.

"Good idea." I nodded. "I prefer the dark when it's light."

"We'll check our traps tomorrow morning," said Gabby, rolling over in her sleeping bag and cuddling up next to mine. "I really, really hope we've caught a badger."

"Me too," I whispered. "It's a shame we didn't catch any squirrels. We could have tamed them and let them sleep with us tonight in our tent. In our actual sleeping bags!"

"I think I'd rather sleep with a rabbit than a squirrel," said Gabby. "I think squirrels' tails would be far too tickly!"

"LIGHTS OFF, GIRLS!" Gabby's dad shouted from the orange tent next door. "Less chatting, more sleeping please!"

The **trouble with less chatting, more sleeping** is, chatting is much more fun than going to sleep. Especially if you're cuddling up with your best friend in an actual sleeping bag in an actual tent in the actual woods under the actual stars!

So we changed our chatting to whispering instead.

And we left our light on. (So we could see each other's faces.)

"Jack Beechwhistle will be soooooo jealous if we take a badger to school on Monday," I whispered.

"He'll probably cry like a baby!" Gabby giggled. "Lots of the animals we're trying to catch are nocturnal, so I'm sure we'll definitely have a really good chance of catching something while it's dark."

"What's nocturnal?" I whispered.

"It means you're an animal that mainly comes out at night," she whispered back. "And mainly sleeps during the day. Badgers are nocturnal, foxes are nocturnal, hedgehogs are nocturnal . . . I'm not sure about rabbits and squirrels."

"So some nocturnal nature could be sniffing our carrot right now!" I whispered excitedly.

"And our peanuts," said Gabby. "And our chicken nuggets!"

When I realized that a load of nocturnal nature might already be trapped in our traps, I found it even harder to go to sleep!

Or whisper!

Or turn the light off.

"I'm never going to be able to get to sleep now," I whispered. "I can't even close my eyes! I can't even half close them!"

"Do you want to play the alphabet game with me?" whispered Gabby.

"What's the alphabet game?" I whispered back.

"It's a game about alphabets," whispered Gabby. "For example, I say the name of some nature that begins with A, like antelope."

"Or adder!" I whispered.

"Exactly," said Gabby. "Then, if we both get an A, we move on to B, and then to C, all the way to Z, thinking of different types of nature."

"I can only think of zebra," I said, jumping ahead a bit.

"I usually fall asleep before I get

to Z," whispered Gabby.

"Can I start?" I whispered, because I'd already thought of a really good B.

"OK," Gabby whispered back.

"Bee," I whispered.

"Badger!" Gabby whispered back.

"Cow," I whispered.

"Caterpillar!" Gabby whispered back.

"Deer," whispered Gabby.

"Dragon," I giggled back.

"Elephant."

"Excellent other type of animal," I whispered.

"You can't have that!" said Gabby, totally forgetting to whisper.

"LIGHTS OFF!" shouted Gabby's dad.

Thank goodness I'd brought my three-colour torch.

CHAPTER 20

Camping in Potts Wood with Gabby and her dad on Saturday WAS THE ABSOLUTE BEST!

Well, it was the absolute best until we woke up on Sunday morning.

When I opened my eyes yesterday morning, not only had the batteries in my three-colour torch run out, but the front bit of our tent had collapsed! And the middle!

PEEEEEEEEEEEEEEEEEEEEEEEEEEEEEEEEEEEEEEEEEEP! I peeped, blowing my emergency whistle as hard as I could.

PEEEEEEEEEEEEEEEEEEEEEEEEEEEEEEEEE EEEEEEEEEEEEEEEEEEEEEEEEEEP! peeped Gabby, jumping up in her sleeping bag, seeing what I was seeing and blowing her whistle even harder.

The **trouble with the front bit and the middle bit of your tent collapsing in the night** is, you can't see any way to get out! All you can see in front of you is collapsed tent!!

PEEEEEEEEEEEEEEEEEEEEEEEEEEEEEEEEEE EEEEEEEEEEEEEEEEEEEEEEEEEEEEEEEEEEEE EEEEEEEEEEEEEP! we both peeped, and kept peeping until we heard Gabby's dad coming to the rescue.

"COMING, GIRLS!" he shouted, undoing the zip of our collapsed lounge, and crawling on his tummy into our half-collapsed bedroom.

"DON'T PANIC!" he shouted. "The air has come out of the front and middle supports," he puffed. "Nothing to worry about at all!"

Gabby and I were so busy worrying about not having anything to worry about that we didn't even notice the air had gone out of our inflatable sleeping mats too.

"Goodness me," panted Gabby's dad as he wriggled into our tent to rescue us.

"I didn't burst it," said Gabby.

"I didn't burst it either," I said.

The **trouble with telling a grown-up you haven't burst something** is, you can never be sure they believe you. Especially if you are the nearest ones to a bursting tent when it bursts.

"Maybe a hedgehog bumped into us in the night," whispered Gabby as her dad started deflating the only part of our tent that wasn't already flat.

"Or a porcupine," I whispered. "Maybe a herd of nocturnal porcupines smelled our doughnuts, stampeded into us in the dark and burst everything."

"I don't think we'll tell my dad that though," said Gabby. "He looks a bit busy at the moment. Maybe we should just go and check our traps."

"The TRAPS!"

I gasped.

"I'd forgotten all about the traps!"

As soon as Gabby's dad had got control of our flat tent, we raced off to see how many animals we had caught in the night.

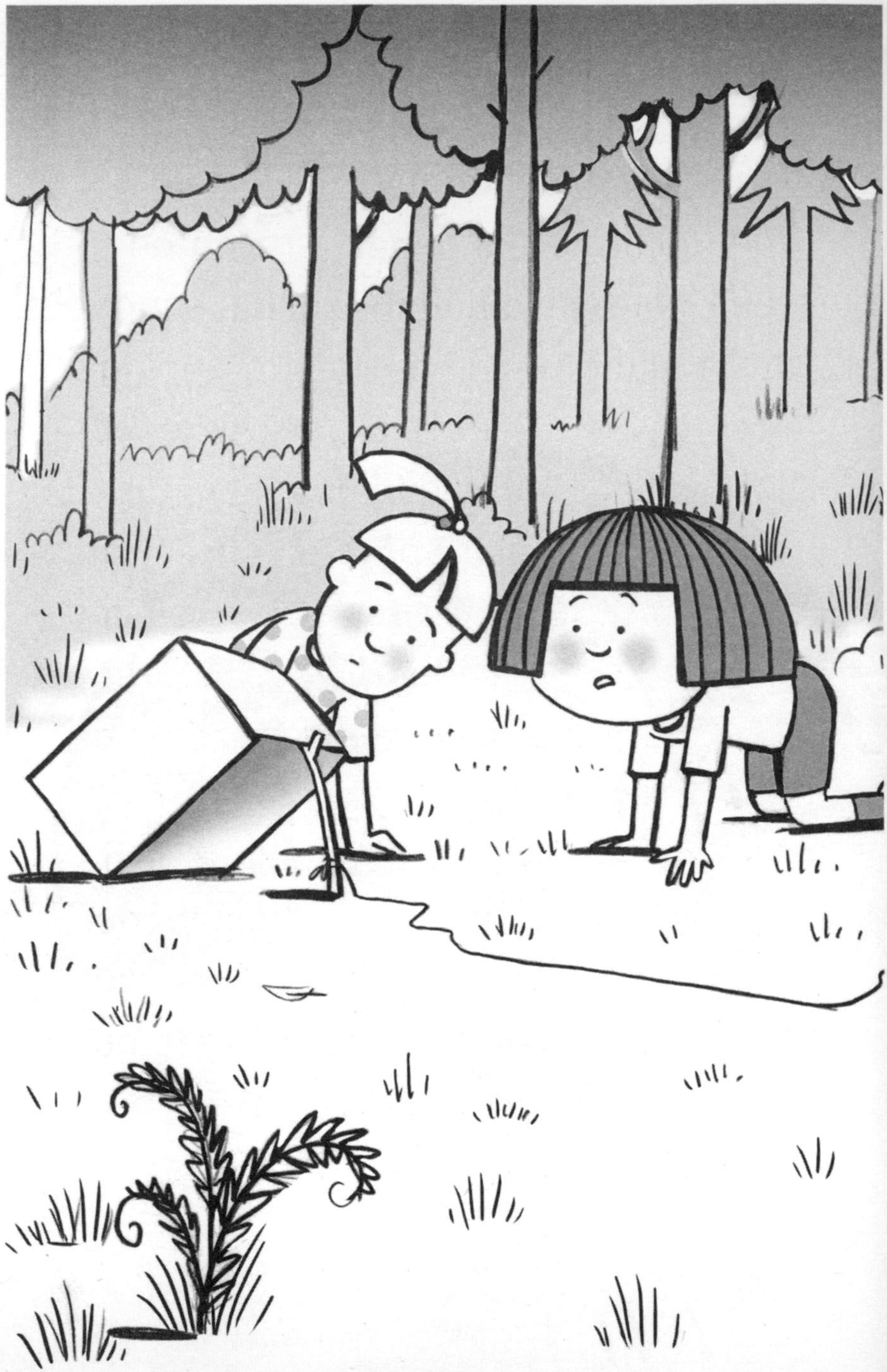

It was more bad news.

Our carrot had gone.

Trouble is, so had the rabbit.

We did find some rabbit droppings near to where the carrot used to be, but neither of us wanted to pick them up.

"All our other traps are just as we left them!" sighed Gabby, pulling all the strings to double-check they worked. "I felt sure we were going to catch at least a fox."

"Maybe the fox caught all the rabbits before they could get to our traps," I said. "And the squirrels and the badgers. What are we going to put in our school nature garden now?"

"What about some whittled sticks?" Gabby suggested.

"Maybe not," I said. "Teachers don't

like pointy ends."

"Oh well, it was fun trying!" said Gabby. "Looking for nature is such fun!"

"How far did we get in the alphabet game?" I asked. "I think I fell asleep."

"Manatee," said Gabby.

"Manatee?" I frowned. "What's a manatee?!"

"It's like an underwater sea cow that kind of floats around eating sea cabbage and sea greens."

"What about sea peas?" I asked.

"Probably," said Gabby, dropping one of her animal traps and stopping to pick it up.

"No wonder I fell asleep," I said. "I'm not sure I'd want a manatee in our nature garden."

By the time we had carried our traps back to our tent, neither of the tents were there. Well, they were kind of there, only Gabby's dad had rolled them up really tightly and packed them back in their bags.

Three trips to the car and we were ready to go home.

"Goodbye, Potts Wood!" said Gabby as we climbed into the car with a wave. "Sorry we couldn't take any of you home with us."

"Wait! I've left something behind!" I said suddenly, unclipping my seat belt and racing back down the track. "I'm just going to get it."

"What did you forget?" asked Gabby as I raced back to the car and climbed in beside her.

"Wood ants!" I whispered.

CHAPTER 21

The **trouble with wood ants** is, you're not really meant to take them to school. Especially in your lunch box.

But I did. Because no one at my school would have seen wood ants before. They would only have seen normal ants.

Trouble is, it was raining.

And raining

and raining!

The **trouble with rain that rains and rains and rains** is, as soon as it starts, teachers think you're going to dissolve. So instead of letting me run straight over to the nature garden to set my wood ants free, they made me run straight to my classroom.

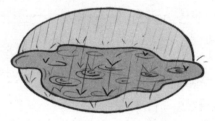

What are you going to do now? Gabby asked me in a secret note during Geography.

Wait till morning break, I told her in a secret note back.

What if it's still raining during morning break? she asked me in another secret note during History.

It better not be, I wrote back.

But it was.

"We're going to be stuck inside till lunchtime now!" I grumbled. "Even if it stops raining, we'll still have to go and eat our sandwiches first."

"You haven't got any sandwiches," whispered Gabby. "You've only got wood ants."

"I know," I whispered back.

"What are you going to do?" whispered Gabby.

"I don't know." I shrugged. "I'm still thinking."

By the time the lunch bell rang, the only thing I could think of was to race to the canteen, pretend to gobble my lunch and dash out to the nature garden with Gabby as fast as I could.

Trouble is, dinner ladies were on patrol.

The **trouble with dinner ladies being on patrol** is, they watch your every move.

"Where are your sandwiches, Daisy?" asked Mrs Keble with a really suspicious frown.

"I ate them really quickly," I said.

"Where's your lunch box, Daisy?" asked Mrs Keble.

"In my school bag," I said.

"Shouldn't your lunch box be on the table?" she said.

"Not today, no."

"No apple today, Daisy?"

"Not today, no."

"No yoghurt today, Daisy?"

"Not today, no."

"Go and fetch your lunch box please."

"Do I have to?"

"Yes, you do."

"Open your lunch box please, Daisy."

"I'd rather not."

"Give me your lunch box please, Daisy."

"Do I have to?"

"Yes, you do."

"Do I *really* have to?"

"Yes, you really, *really* have to," Mrs Keble said.

So I did.

The **trouble with giving a dinner lady your lunch box** is, it can make them scream if they open it. And drop the box.

Especially if it's full of wood ants.

As soon as Mrs Keble dropped my lunch box, my wood ants went everywhere. So did all the little twigs they were living in. They went on the table, they went on the floor, they went on Nishta Bagwhat's Scotch egg, they went all over Mrs Keble's shoes.

The **trouble with wood ants and wood-ant twigs going everywhere** is, it didn't just make Mrs Keble scream, it made *all* the dinner ladies scream.

And all the children in the canteen. Even Gabby screamed, and she had known about my wood ants all along.

I didn't say anything though. I didn't want Gabby to get into trouble too.

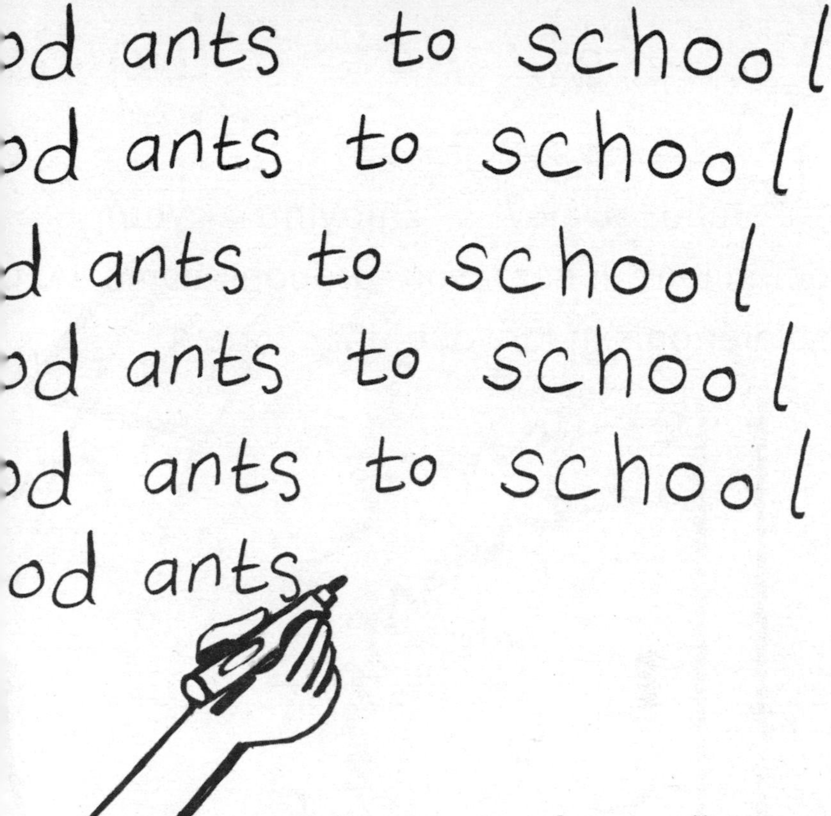

od ants   to school
od ants to school
d ants to school
od ants to school
od ants to school
od ants

Talk about unfair – all I was
trying to do was put some
super-sized actual nature in our
super-boring nature garden. How was I
supposed to know a dinner lady would
totally go and ruin things?

"Hello, Daisy! Enjoying your detention? I hear you brought some soldier ants in for your lunch today!"

"They weren't soldier ants. They were wood ants."

"Did you have a nice time camping on Saturday?"

"See any adders while you were camping?"

"No, we didn't."

"Hear any adders while you were camping?"

"No, we didn't."

"Are you sure? I definitely heard some hisses when I was out on my bike in Potts Wood on Saturday night. The pin on my secret agent badge heard them too . . .

. . . HISSSSSSSSSSSSSSSSSSSSSSSSSSSSSSS
SSSSSSSSSSSSSSSSSSSSSSSSSSSSSSSSSSSSSS
SSSSSSSSSSSSSSSSSSS!"

He wouldn't.

Would he?

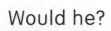

He couldn't.

Could he?

HE DIDN'T?

DID HE?

He DID!

GRRRRRRRRRRRRRR!!!!!

DAISY'S
TROUBLE INDEX

The trouble with . . .

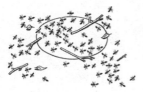

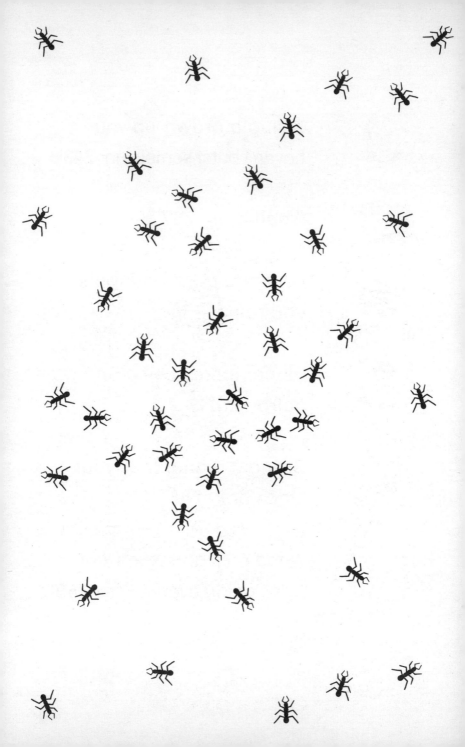